Silly Rhymes

for

Silly Times

a collection of
limericks by

Andy Statham
and
Alan Dickson

with illustrations by
Janet Ewing &
Alan Dickson

This book is dedicated to all of the silly people out there ... make some noise.

I always thought FARMING was nice

So I started with goats and some rice

But the goats ate the grain

And became quite insane

And now they all ride round on bikes

I used to deliver the post

Until I encountered a ghost

It told me its story

So bloody and gory

That now I post post as a ghost.

Something I've wanted to do
Was to talk to an owl that I knew
I started to stutter
And then tried to utter
T-t-t-t-t twit twoo

An inventor I am, and you'll hear
Of the plane that I made with a gear,
That made it take flight
So much faster than light
That it came back the previous year

A Scot with a Canada goose
Once lived in a very big hoose
One night from the attic
Came sounds quite traumatic
Turned out there's a moose in the hoose

SCIENCE was always my **thing**

I discovered that **frogs** always *sing*

When brought to the **boil**

In *garlic* and OIL

So I opened a shop in **Peking**

While enjoying some tea with my nieces

We chopped up my sister in pieces

We cut off her head

Then her arms and her legs

Now she looks like an alien species

There was an old warlock called Fred
Who woke up one morning quite dead
He brewed up a spell
With a terrible smell
And now he's a Zombie instead

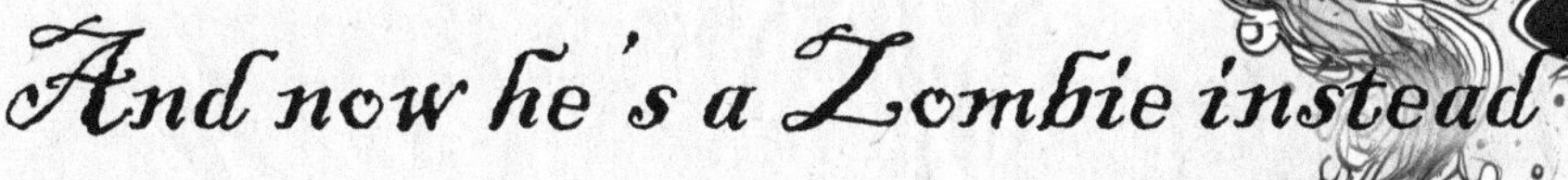

One day I had nothing to do
So took up a job in the zoo
I cleaned out the apes
The tigers, the snakes
And ended up covered in poo

Admiring the moon and the stars

I dreamt I was going to Mars

But a clown on a bike

Took an instant **DISLIKE**

To my cat as it played the **Guitar**

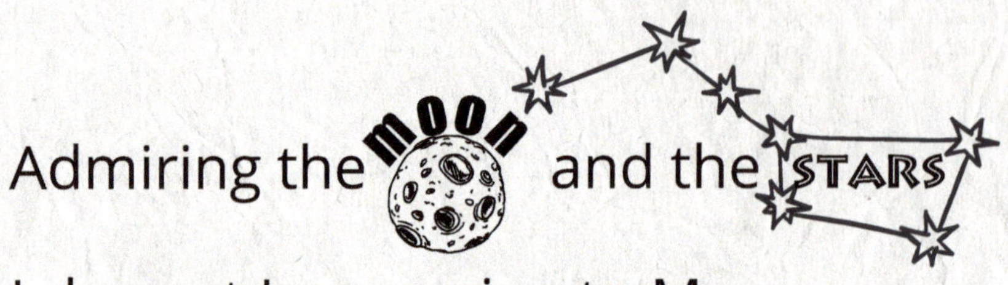

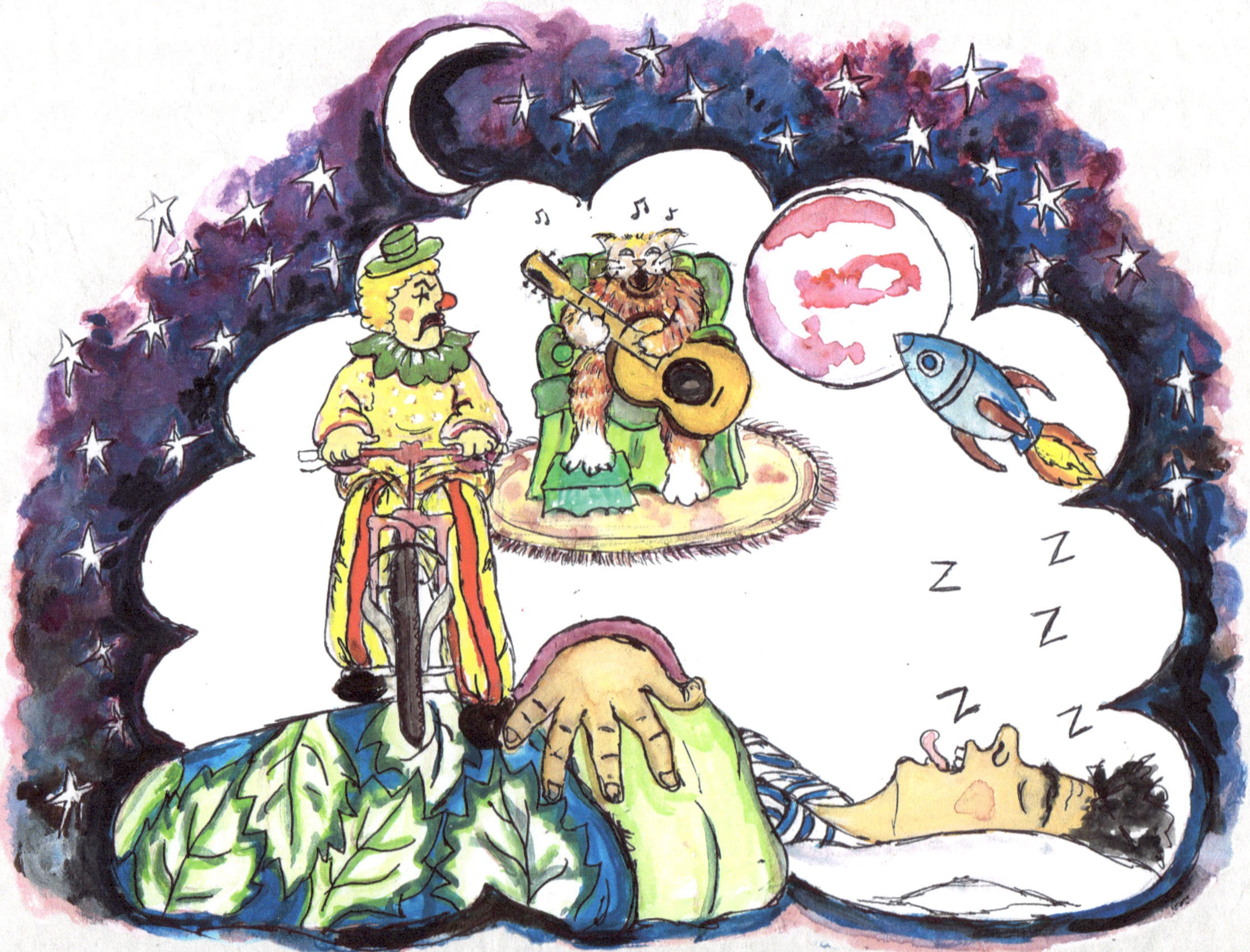

A snake with a poisonous bite
Took a room at an inn for a night
Where the hippo next door
Played the bugle till 4
When the snake stopped the noise with one bite

A hippo who loved eating beans
And copious helpings of greens
One night with a start
Gave a huge smelly fart
That emptied the pond of sardines

An elephant wearing a **WIG**
Was happily stuffing a pig
With chocolate and **CUSTARD**,
And lashings of mustard
And delicate pieces of fig

I once played guitar in a band
'Til the day that I severed my hand
With a circular saw
That I found on the floor
It wasn't quite what I had planned

A hippo was stuck in the loo
And didn't know what she should do
They pushed from above
With one mighty shove
And she ended up back in the zoo

An outspoken Scottish librarian
Told a lion it was a barbarian,
"You shouldn't eat meat,
You know it's not reet."
Now the lion's a strict vegetarian

With a swing of his sword the old knight

Gave the woman a terrible fright

As the blade cut the air

It severed her hair

And caused her pet cat to ignite

Two unicorns went to the ark
And boarded the ship after dark
"We've not met before"
"Delighted I'm sure
I'm Roger and you must be Mark"

A PARROT CAME HERE FROM THE EAST
AND CHATTED TO FRIENDS AT A FEAST
THEY FED HIM ON SNAILS
AND TOENAILS OF WHALES
NOW THE BIRD FROM THE EAST IS DECEASED

Morris was teasing the crows

Most silly as everyone knows

They pecked out his eyes

Despite all his cries

But didn't much care for his nose

A gentleman wanted the 

He needed a big # 

He looked at his hat

And thought I'll use that

And now it is full of his

Some friends that were riding on bikes

On tandems and some were on trikes

At Instagram spots

They took many shots

Just hoping for plenty of likes

I once got a leg in the post
And thought it was something to roast
It turned on the spit
And I have to admit
It turned out more tasty than most

Cooking a cat is an art
Said the dog as he cut one apart
I like them with chilli
And though it sounds silly
I've never put one in a tart

A CROCODILE CALLED UNCLE SNAPPY
WAS FOUND TO BE AT HIS MOST HAPPY
WHEN CRUNCHING ON BONES
AND IGNORING THE MOANS
OF THE PEOPLE WHO'D MADE HIM UNHAPPY

I often think giraffes are quite tall
And mice are incredibly small
And squirrels are bushy
And frogs are quite mooshy
And rhinos don't do much at all

A HEDGEHOG WAS ROLLED IN A BALL
WHEN HE FELT HIMSELF STARTING TO FALL
HE ROLLED DOWN A HILL
FELT DECIDEDLY ILL
AND SPLATTERED HIMSELF ON A WALL

A starving young vegan from Crete

Was looking for something to eat

On passing a store

Selling chickens galore

Said, "**** it" I'm eating some meat.
Dang
Darn
Blast
Stuff
Blow
Drat
****

Desiree, a cat very smart
Drove round on the greengrocer's cart
She nibbled on beans
And all sorts of greens
And smiled as she let off huge farts

"make some noise"

www.ingramcontent.com/pod-product-compliance
Lightning Source LLC
Chambersburg PA
CBHW042138110726
48006CB00003B/917